# THE WIZARD OF OZ

Illustrated by
GREG HILDEBRANDT

Adapted from the novel by
L. Frank Baum

The Unicorn Publishing House
New Jersey

# THE WIZARD OF OZ

orothy lived in the middle of the great Kansas prairie with her Uncle Henry and Aunt Em. Their house was only one room. The house had no attic and no cellar. There was only a small hole dug in the ground. This was called a cyclone cellar. The family could go down there in case one of those great whirlwinds arose.

When Dorothy looked outside the house, she could see nothing but the great *gray* prairie on all sides. The sun and the wind had baked the land into a gray mass with little cracks running through it. Not a tree or house appeared across the flat countryside.

Aunt Em had come there when she was a young, pretty wife. The sun and wind had changed her, too. They had taken the sparkle from her eyes and left them a dark gray. She was thin and tired, and never smiled now. When Dorothy, who was an orphan, first came, Aunt Em would look at the little girl with wonder that she could find anything at all to laugh at.

Uncle Henry never laughed. He was gray also, from his long beard to his rough boots. He looked stern and grave, and rarely spoke.

It was Toto that saved Dorothy from growing as gray as everything else. Toto was a small black dog with long silky hair who played all day long, and he was Dorothy's only friend.

But today they were not playing. Uncle Henry was looking fearfully at the sky. It was grayer than usual. Dorothy stood looking at the sky, too. Aunt Em was busy washing the dishes. Far away, they heard the low wail of the wind.

Suddenly, Uncle Henry said, "There's a cyclone coming, Em. I'll go look after the stock." Then he ran to the sheds where the cows and horses were kept.

Aunt Em dropped her work and came to the door. One

glance told her of the danger close at hand. "Quick, Dorothy!" she screamed, "run for the cellar!"

Dorothy grabbed up Toto, but he jumped out of her arms and hid under the bed. She ran over to the bed to get him. Aunt Em, badly frightened, threw open the trapdoor in the floor and climbed down the ladder into the small, dark hole. Dorothy caught Toto at last and started to follow her aunt. When she was halfway across the room, there was a great shriek from the wind. The house shook so hard that she sat down suddenly on the floor.

A strange *thing* then happened.

The house whirled around two or three times and then rose slowly through the air. It rose to the top of the cyclone and there it stayed. It was carried miles and miles away as easily as you can carry a feather.

It was very dark, and the wind howled horribly around her, but Dorothy found she was riding quite smoothly. After the first few whirls around, she felt as if she were being rocked gently, like a baby in a cradle.

Hour after hour passed away. Dorothy slowly got over her fright, but she felt quite lonely. At first she wondered if she would be dashed to pieces when the house fell again. But as the hours passed and nothing terrible happened, she stopped worrying and resolved to wait calmly. At last she closed her eyes and fell fast asleep.

She was awakened by a shock. She sat up and noticed that the house was no longer moving. It wasn't dark, either. Sunshine now poured into the room. She sprang from her bed and with Toto at her heels ran and opened the door.

The little girl gave a cry of surprise. Her eyes grew big at the wonderful things she saw. The cyclone had set the house down in the middle of a beautiful country. All about her were trees with rich with fruit, and patches of emerald green grass.

Then she saw a group of very strange people coming toward her. There were three men who were about as tall as Dorothy, and with them an old woman dressed in white. The

woman's dress was sprinkled with tiny stars. They looked just like diamonds. The men were all dressed in blue from head to toe. They all wore large pointed hats.

"I am the Good Witch of the North," said the old woman. "I welcome you to the land of Oz. You are a heroine, for when your house fell, it landed on the Wicked Witch of the East. You have set the Munchkins free from her. Now there is only one wicked witch left in all of Oz: the Wicked Witch of the West."

Dorothy looked where the Witch pointed. Underneath her house were two feet sticking out, wearing Silver Shoes. One of the Munchkins handed the shoes to the Witch. She gave them to Dorothy. "These *magical* shoes are now yours," the little woman said, "but what magic they can do, I do not know."

Dorothy asked if the magic might help her to go home.

"There is a great desert all around Oz," said the Witch. "The only one who could help you return home is the Great Wizard, Oz, who lives in the Emerald City. He is a wizard who can take any form he wishes. It is a long trip, but the road to the City of Emeralds is paved with yellow brick, so you cannot miss it." She kissed Dorothy gently on the forehead. Where her lips touched, they left a shining mark. "I have given you my kiss, and no one will dare to hurt a person who has my mark. Good-bye, my dear." The Munchkins bowed to Dorothy and walked away. The Witch smiled and disappeared.

Dorothy went into the house and packed some bread in a basket. She put on a clean dress and then looked at her worn shoes. "These will never do for a long trip, Toto," she said. She tried on the silver slippers. They fit her as if they were made for her. She grabbed up her basket and was off down the yellow brick road.

She found the country very pretty. The houses of the Munchkins were very odd looking, as they were all round and painted blue. In that country, blue was the favorite color. Toward evening, when Dorothy grew tired, she stopped at a large house. There was a party on the lawn, and the Munchkins greeted Dorothy and invited her to pass the night

with them. Dorothy ate a big supper and went out to watch the Munchkins dance. Five little fiddlers were playing as loudly as possible. Munchkins were talking, laughing, and singing. There was a big table outside with cakes and pies and nuts and fruits. When Dorothy was tired of watching the dance, they led her off to bed. Even the sheets were blue. Dorothy crawled in and slept with Toto by her feet.

The next day, she bade her new friends good-bye. Again she set off down the yellow brick road. When she had gone several miles, she sat down on a fence to rest. She looked up at a Scarecrow, who was propped up on a pole. He was dressed in an old suit of Munchkin clothes and wore an old pointed hat.

As Dorothy looked at the queer painted face of the Scarecrow, she was surprised as one of his eyes winked at her.

"Good-day," said the Scarecrow, in a rather husky voice.

"Good-day," said Dorothy in surprise. "Can't you get down from there?"

"No," said the Scarecrow, "for this pole is stuck up my back. If you *could* take me down, I would be most thankful."

Dorothy lifted the straw man off the pole. "My name is Dorothy," she said. "I am going to the Emerald City to ask the great Wizard of Oz to send me home to Kansas."

"Do you think," asked the Scarecrow, "that the Wizard might give me some brains if I asked? You see, my head is stuffed with straw." Toto sniffed at the straw man.

"I cannot say," said Dorothy, "but come with me and ask."

"I will," said the Scarecrow. "You see, I don't mind having arms and legs of straw. I cannot get hurt. But I don't like being called a fool. And without brains you *are* a fool."

They went back to the road and started walking. Toward night, they came to a great wood and spent the night in a deserted cabin. Dorothy lay down at once. Then Toto lay down beside her, and they soon fell asleep. The Scarecrow, who was never tired, stood in a corner of the room and waited until morning came.

When Dorothy awoke, the sun was shining brightly. They set

off walking through the woods. Suddenly, Dorothy gave a cry of surprise. In front of them stood a man made of tin. He stood quite still with his axe held high, as if he were about to chop down the tree before him.

"Please get an oilcan and oil my joints," squeaked the Tin Man. "They have rusted so much, I can't move at all!"

Dorothy thought she had seen an oilcan back at the cabin. She quickly ran back to get it. Returning, she set to work oiling the Tin Man's joints, till at last he could move again.

"Thank you," said the Tin Man. "You have saved me. I have been standing by this tree for years."

"What happened to you?" asked the Scarecrow.

"I was out cutting trees one day when a storm suddenly broke. Foolishly, I ignored the danger. I just kept right on chopping as the rain fell. And as I drew my axe back, I froze. It was then that I knew I had rusted stiff, but it was too late. I might never have moved again if it wasn't for you. But what brought you here to these woods?"

"We were on our way to see the Wizard of Oz," Dorothy said. "This is the Scarecrow. He is going to ask the Wizard for some brains. My name is Dorothy. I'm going to ask him to send me back home."

"Do you think he would *give* me a heart?" asked the Tin Man. "You see, the tinsmith who made me forgot to give me one."

"I've been told he is a very great wizard," Dorothy said. "And if he can give the Scarecrow some brains, then surely he would be able to give you a heart."

"Come along, Tin Man," said the Scarecrow, cheerfully. And the Tin Man happily agreed.

As the friends walked along, the woods became deeper and darker. From behind the trees came strange and frightening growls. The Scarecrow and the Tin Man walked on each side of Dorothy, ready to protect her from what might be lurking in the dark forest.

Suddenly, a huge Lion jumped out from a tree. With one

blow from his paw, he sent the Scarecrow spinning into the air. Then he knocked the Tin Man down into the road.

Little Toto ran forward, barking with all his might. The Lion opened his mouth to bite him. Dorothy didn't stop to think about the danger. She stepped right up in front of the Lion and slapped him on the nose.

"Don't you *dare* bite Toto!" she cried.

"I didn't bite him!" said the Lion, shaking with fright. "You didn't have to hit me."

"Why, you're nothing but a big coward!" said Dorothy. She was surprised, for the Lion was very big.

"I know," said the Cowardly Lion, hanging his head in shame. "And it makes me so sad."

"Why are you a coward?" asked Dorothy.

"I don't know," replied the Lion. "I suppose I was born this way. All the other animals think that I'm brave. If I should ever have to fight, I would run away, for you see, I have no courage." The Lion wiped a tear away with his tail.

"Why don't you come with us to see the Wizard of Oz?" Dorothy asked. "Perhaps he could *give* you courage."

"If you'll have me," said the Lion, meekly. "Life is simply awful without a bit of courage."

So the new friends set off along the yellow brick road. As they went along, the woods became even thicker and darker. The Lion whispered to them to watch out for the Kalidahs.

"What are Kalidahs?" asked Dorothy.

"They are frightful beasts with bodies like bears and heads like tigers. I'm very afraid of the Kalidahs!" The Lion shook as he spoke and jumped a little whenever a queer noise rose from the dark forest.

As they walked, the group came to a wide, deep ditch. It was too far to jump. The Tin Man chopped down a tall tree which fell across the gully. They had just started to cross the tree bridge when they heard a dreadful roar behind them.

"There are two Kalidahs!" cried the Lion. "Quick! We must cross at once or we will be killed!"

Dorothy crossed first, followed by the Tin Man and the Scarecrow. Even though he was afraid, the Lion turned to face the monsters and roared. They paused in fear, and the Lion crossed the tree. But seeing they were bigger than the Lion, the Kalidahs rushed forward. As they began to cross the bridge, the Tin Man ran forward and chopped the tree in two.

The Kalidahs fell with a crash into the gully. Both were dashed to pieces on the sharp rocks below.

The group walked on, but they had wandered off the road. Soon they came to a wide river, and shouts of joy arose from the group. For on the other side of the river they could see the yellow brick road that led to Oz.

The Tin Man took up his axe and began to build a raft. When he had finished, they all climbed on board. The Tin Man and the Scarecrow used long poles to push the raft along. Though the current was strong, they soon found themselves safely on the other side and on their way to the Emerald City.

They walked along happily, looking at the lovely flowers all over the ground. There were big yellow and white blossoms. Beside them there were a great number of red poppies. As they walked further on, there were more and more poppies and fewer of the other flowers.

Now it is well known that when there are many of these flowers together, their smell is very strong. Anyone who breathes in their fragrance falls asleep. If the sleeper is not carried away from the flowers, the sleep will last forever. But Dorothy did not know this and soon found her eyes growing heavy. She felt she *simply* had to lie down and sleep a bit. Her eyes closed in spite of herself. She forgot where she was and soon fell fast asleep. Understanding the danger, the Scarecrow told the Lion to run ahead. Then he and the Tin Man picked up Dorothy and Toto and carried them to safety. When they were almost out of the poppy field, they found the Lion sound asleep in the poppies. The flowers had been too strong for their huge friend.

"We can do nothing for him," said the Tin Man. "He is far

too heavy for us to ever lift him away from the poppies. We must leave him here to sleep forever. Perhaps he will *dream* that he has found his courage at last."

"I am sorry. He was a good friend," said the Scarecrow.

They carried Dorothy and Toto away from the deadly smell of the poppies. As the two tended to Dorothy and Toto, they heard a low growl nearby. The Tin Man saw a great yellow wildcat chasing a little gray field mouse. Even though the Tin Man had no heart, he felt it was wrong for the wildcat to kill such a helpless creature. Raising his axe, he killed the wildcat.

The little field mouse drew near and said in a squeaky little voice: "Oh, thank you ever so much for saving my life! I am the queen of all the field mice. Let my subjects repay your brave deed by granting you a wish."

The Scarecrow quickly spoke up: "Perhaps you can help us save our friend, the Lion, who is lying asleep in the poppies. The Tin Man can make a cart. If you would allow us, we could tie all of your subjects to it and carry our friend to safety."

The Queen gave the order, and shortly after, thousands of mice appeared. The mice pulled the Tin Man's cart through the field and out into the fresh air. When Dorothy awoke, the Scarecrow told her what had happened and how the mice had saved the Lion.

The friends sat down to wait for the Lion to wake up. The Lion woke with a loud yawn and a great shake of his mane. When he was fully awake, they set off around the poppy field until they once again found the yellow brick road.

Nothing could be prettier. The country all around them was a bright, cheery green. Soon they came to a pretty little farmhouse. The people outside were all dressed in green.

"We must be very close to the Emerald City," said Dorothy.

"Yes," said the Scarecrow. "Everything in this land is green."

A kind lady invited them to stay the night in her home. In the morning they set out again, and before long they saw a lovely green city rising up just ahead.

"There it is!" cried the Tin Man, pointing. "There is the

Emerald City!" And they all ran as quickly as they could until they came to a great green wall that stood around the city.

In front of them was a big gate. There was a bell beside the gate, and Dorothy stepped up and rang it. A little man about the size of a Munchkin appeared.

"I am the Guardian of the Gates. What is it you wish in the Emerald City?" he asked.

"We want to see the Wizard," said Dorothy.

The man seemed surprised at this answer. "It's been many years since anyone asked to see the Great Oz. I will take you to his palace, but you must first put on green glasses."

"Why *must* we wear glasses?" asked Dorothy.

"Because if you do not wear them, the brightness of the Emerald City will blind you. Everyone in the city must wear glasses day and night. Oz has ordered it."

The Guardian of the Gates opened a big box filled with glasses. He put them on Dorothy and her friends. He even put them on Toto. Then he opened the gates and led them in.

Even with the glasses on, Dorothy and her friends were dazzled by the brightness of the city. The pavement was made of blocks of green marble, joined by rows of shining emeralds. Even the beautiful houses that lined the streets were made of green marble and decorated with emeralds.

There were many people walking about; all dressed in green. They looked at Dorothy with wide eyes.

The Guardian of the Gates led them to a big building in the middle of the city. This was the palace of the Great Wizard.

The friends were led to rooms where they could rest before seeing the Great Wizard. Dorothy's room had a fine bed with green sheets and a green cover. Her closet was filled with beautiful green dresses made of silk, satin, and velvet.

The next day, a soldier with green whiskers appeared. "The Great Oz will see you. But each must see him alone."

Dorothy put on one the prettiest dresses from her closet. Then she boldly went to the throne room. She stood before a great throne made of green marble and covered in emeralds.

But Dorothy didn't look at the beautiful chair. Her eyes fixed on the object that floated just above it. It was a huge head—a head without a body! As Dorothy stared at the strange sight, the head looked down at her. Then it spoke: "I am Oz the Great and Terrible. Who are *you* and why are *you* here?"

Dorothy took courage and said: "*I* am Dorothy the Small and Meek. I want you to send me home to Kansas."

"If you wish me to send you home, you must do something for me. Kill the Wicked Witch of the West. Then I will send you home."

"But I cannot!" cried Dorothy.

"That is my answer," said the Wizard. "Until the Wicked Witch dies, you will not see your home again. Now go!"

Sadly, Dorothy left and went back to her friends.

The next day, the soldier with green whiskers brought the Scarecrow to the throne room. Inside was a lovely lady sitting on the throne. She was dressed in green silk. She looked at the Scarecrow sweetly and said: "I am Oz the Great and Terrible. Who are you and why do you seek me?"

Now the Scarecrow was expecting to see the great head that Dorothy had told him about. He was very surprised. He bowed as prettily as his stuffing would let him.

"I'm only a scarecrow stuffed with straw," the Scarecrow answered; "therefore I have no brains, and I come to you praying that you will put brains in my head, instead of straw."

"I never grant favors without return," said Oz, "but if you kill the Wicked Witch of the West I will give you brains. Until she is dead I will not grant your wish. Now go and earn the brains you ask for."

"I thought that you asked Dorothy to kill the Witch," said the Scarecrow.

"Oz doesn't care who kills the Wicked Witch. Now go."

The Scarecrow left and told his friends what Oz had said.

The following day the Tin Man went to see the Wizard. He found Oz in the form of a great monster. It was huge, with five arms and five eyes. Oz gave the Tin Man the same answer: kill

the Wicked Witch.

The last to see Oz was the Cowardly Lion. Oz appeared to the Lion as a great ball of fire. The Lion begged him for courage, but Oz again demanded he kill the Wicked Witch. Only then would his wish be granted.

The four friends finally decided that they had to do as Oz asked: they had to try to kill the Wicked Witch of the West. The next day, they left the Emerald City and traveled west.

Dorothy still wore the pretty silk dress she had put on in the palace, but to her surprise it turned pure white when they left the city.

The Emerald City was soon left far behind. It was a hot trip, for there were no trees to offer them shade. By afternoon they decided to stop for a rest. Dorothy, Toto, and the Lion soon fell fast asleep on the soft grass. The Tin Man and the Scarecrow remained standing and kept watch over their friends.

Now the Wicked Witch of the West had only one eye, but that eye was as strong as a telescope. She could see everywhere. So as she looked out into the distance she saw Dorothy and her friends sleeping.

They were a long way off, but the Wicked Witch was angry to find them in her domain. She jumped up and blew a silver whistle that hung around her neck. At once, a great pack of wolves came running to her from all directions.

"Go to those people," said the Witch. "Tear them to pieces."

"Are you *not* going to make them slaves?" asked the leader of the wolves.

"No," she answered. "None of them is fit to work, so you may tear them into small pieces."

"Very well," said the wolf.

The Scarecrow and the Tin Man heard the wolves coming.

"This is *my* fight," said the Tin Man; "so get behind me and I will meet them as they come." He took his axe and killed the leader of the wolves as he approached. There were forty wolves in all, and one after another fell before the Tin Man. He stood his ground until at last all lay in a heap before him.

Dorothy was quite frightened when she woke up and saw the great pile of shaggy wolves. The Tin Man told her what had happened and they started once again on their trip.

The Wicked Witch looked out with her far-seeing eye and saw her wolves lying dead. She stamped her foot and tore at her hair. Then she called for twelve of her slaves. They were the Winkies. The Winkies were not a brave people, but they had to do as they were told.

The Winkies timidly marched away until they came to Dorothy and her friends. The Lion gave a great roar, terrifying the Winkies. They ran back as fast as their little legs could carry them. The Witch sat down to think of what to do next.

There was, in her cupboard, a Golden Cap, which had a strange magical power. Whoever owned it could call three times upon the Winged Monkeys. They would obey any orders that were given. Twice before the Wicked Witch had used the charm of the Cap: once to make the Winkies her slaves and once to drive the Great Oz out of the land of the West.

She put the Cap on her head. There was a rushing of many wings, and the Winged Monkeys appeared before the Witch.

"Go to the strangers within my land and destroy them," she said. "But don't kill the Lion. I will use him like a horse and make him work."

One monkey, much bigger than the others, flew close to the Witch, saying: "You have called us for the third and last time. Your orders will be obeyed." There was a great deal of laughter and chattering and the furious sound of beating wings as they rose in the air. The Winged Monkeys flew at once to the place where Dorothy and her friends were walking.

Some of the Monkeys grabbed the Tin Man. They carried him off till they came over a land thickly covered with sharp rocks. There they dropped him on the rocks where he lay battered and dented. Another group of Monkeys caught the Scarecrow and pulled all the straw out of him. The Monkeys then threw thick pieces of rope around the Lion. They lifted him up and flew away to the Witch's castle.

The leader of the Winged Monkeys flew up to Dorothy. He stopped short when he saw the Good Witch's kiss on Dorothy's forehead.

"We dare not *harm* this little girl," he said, "for she is protected by the Power of Good." The Monkeys decided to carry her to the Witch's castle. There they set her and Toto down on the front step.

The Wicked Witch was both surprised and worried when she saw the mark of the Good Witch's kiss. She looked down at Dorothy's feet; and upon seeing the Silver Shoes, she began to shake violently. But then the Witch looked into Dorothy's eyes. She saw that the little girl didn't know of the power that lay in those shoes.

The Witch set Dorothy to work scrubbing the castle. She often threatened to beat her. In truth, the Witch did not dare strike Dorothy, because of the mark of the Good Witch's kiss on her forehead. But the child did not know this.

Now the Witch wanted to own the Silver Shoes very badly. Dorothy never took them off, except at night, and when she took a bath. The Witch was too afraid of the dark to go into Dorothy's room at night. She was even more afraid of water.

But the wicked creature was very smart. She finally thought of a trick to gain the silver slippers. Placing an iron bar in the middle of the floor, she turned it invisible. Dorothy tripped over the bar and one of her shoes came off. The Witch snatched it and placed it on her own skinny foot.

"Give me back my shoe!" demanded Dorothy. The Witch refused. Dorothy grew so angry that she picked up a bucket of water and threw it over the Witch.

Instantly the Witch gave a loud cry of fear and began to melt away!

"See *what* you have done!" she screamed. "In a minute I shall *melt* away to nothing! Gone, gone! Didn't you know that water would be the end of me?"

"Of course not," said Dorothy. "I'm very sorry indeed." The Witch fell down in a brown, melted, shapeless mess.

Finally free, the Winkies called Dorothy a heroine and released the Lion. Then they went out and found the injured Scarecrow and Tin Man. The Winkies stuffed the Scarecrow with nice, clean straw. Then they worked for days hammering, bending, and polishing the Tin Man until he was like new.

Then Dorothy took the Golden Cap and called for the Winged Monkeys to carry them back to the Emerald City. The Guardian of the Gates couldn't believe they had returned. He brought them in at once to see the Wizard.

There came a voice, as if from the top of the room, that said: "I am Oz the Great and Terrible. Have you killed the Wicked Witch?"

"Yes," said Dorothy. "We melted her. Now we have come to have our wishes granted."

"Dear me," said Oz; "how sudden! Come back tomorrow and I will think it over."

"You've had plenty of time!" said the Tin Man.

"We won't wait a day longer!" said the Scarecrow.

The Lion thought it might be a good idea to frighten the Wizard. He gave a loud roar that was so fierce Toto jumped away in alarm. He tipped over a screen that stood in a corner. As it fell with a crash, they saw a little man with a bald head. He seemed as surprised as they were. The Tin Man stepped between the little man and the others.

"Who are you?" the Tin Man demanded.

"I am Oz the Great and Terrible," said the little man with a shaky voice. "Please don't hurt me."

"Aren't you a great Wizard?" asked Dorothy.

"Oh no, my dear," he said; "I have been making believe. I have been a humbug. I'm just a common man. All you and your friends saw were just tricks. Illusions really. Please don't tell anyone that you found me out."

"What about my *brains?*" asked the Scarecrow.

"Or my *heart?*" asked the Tin Man.

"Or my *courage?*" asked the Lion.

"How will I ever get *home?*" asked Dorothy.

"Calm down, my friends. If you come back tomorrow, I shall help you all," said Oz.

The next morning they returned to the throne room. Oz took the Scarecrow's head off, which didn't bother him a bit, and filled it with pins and needles, saying that this would make him "sharp." Next, he cut out a hole in the Tin Man's chest and placed in it a small silk heart. "Is it a kind heart?" asked the Tin Man. "Very much so, my friend, very much," replied Oz. And finally to the Lion he gave a potion he called courage.

"You must drink this," said Oz; "for courage must always be inside one." The Lion drank the potion at once.

"Ah! Now I am full of courage!" the Lion said joyfully, and he went and rejoined his friends.

"In order to go home," Oz said, turning to Dorothy; "we will have to make a big balloon. There is plenty of silk in the Emerald City. We will set to work at once sewing a great hot-air balloon that will carry us over the desert."

"Us?" asked Dorothy. "Are you going?"

"Yes," said the little man. "I'm from Omaha myself. I came here in a balloon, and the people believed me a Wizard. I had them build the Emerald City. I made everyone wear green glasses so that everything they saw looked green."

"But isn't everything here green?" asked Dorothy.

"No more than any other city," said Oz.

Dorothy got a needle and thread. As fast as Oz could cut the strips of silk, Dorothy sewed them together. When the balloon was finished, Oz sent word to his people that he was going to visit his brother Wizards in the sky. Everyone came to see the wonderful sight and bid the Great Oz good-bye.

Oz told the people that the Scarecrow would rule the city while he was away. Then he called for Dorothy to hurry.

"I can't find Toto," cried Dorothy. She searched through the crowd for him. At last she found him barking at a kitten. She picked him up and ran toward the balloon.

When she was within a few steps of the balloon, the ropes holding it down snapped off. "Come back!" she cried.

"I can't," Oz called back. "Good-bye, good-bye, everyone!" And the balloon floated away. "Good-bye!" everyone shouted as they waved. All eyes were watching the basket float higher and higher into the sky. The people would miss their Wizard. That was the last any of them ever saw of the great Oz.

Dorothy wept bitterly at the passing of her hope to get home again. But when she thought it over she was glad; after all, the balloon might well have carried her even further away from Kansas, if that were possible.

The Scarecrow was now ruler of the Emerald City. Even though he was not a Wizard the people were quite proud of him. "For," they said, "there are no other cities in the world ruled by a *stuffed* man."

The next day, the four friends met in the throne room. There they talked among themselves. The Scarecrow was thinking so hard that the pins and needles that Oz had given him for brains stuck out from all over his head.

"Let us send for the soldier with green whiskers," he finally said. "We will ask for his advice on how to get Dorothy home." So the soldier was summoned to the throne room.

"Glinda, the Good Witch of the South, might be able to help you home," said the soldier.

"Where can we find her?" Dorothy asked.

"Her castle is far to the south," replied the soldier, "and the road leading there is full of dangers. There is a race of fierce men who won't let anyone cross their land."

In spite of the dangers the four friends decided to make the journey and ask the Good Witch of the South for help.

The next day, they left the Emerald City. The sun shone brightly as our friends turned their faces toward the land of the South. Dorothy found herself once more filled with hope. She was certain she would find a way home. They walked the entire day and slept that night under the stars.

The following morning they came to a thick wood. The Scarecrow took the lead and walked forward. But as he came upon the first tree, the branches bent down and grabbed him.

The next minute he found himself lifted up and flung high into the air. Luckily, the Scarecrow wasn't hurt a bit, and he stood up and tried again. But right away the tree grabbed him and tossed him back. This time he had grown quite dizzy. Dorothy helped him get back on his feet and brushed him off.

"This is strange," said Dorothy. "What *shall* we do?"

"The trees seem to have made up their minds to fight us," said the Lion.

"I believe I will try it next," said the Tin Man. As a big branch bent down to grab him, the Tin Man chopped it off with his axe.

"Come on!" he shouted to the others.

They all ran forward and passed beneath the tree without getting hurt. The other trees of the forest did nothing to keep them back. They decided that the first tree was probably the policeman of the forest, to keep strangers out of the wood.

They quickly passed through the forest and came upon a steep hill, covered with rocks. The Scarecrow again led the way for the group. They had nearly reached the first rock when they heard a rough voice cry out: "Keep back! This hill belongs to us and we don't allow anyone to cross over it."

Then from behind a rock stepped the strangest little man. He was quite short and stout and had a big head that was flat at the top. His thick neck was full of wrinkles with a hairy body that was without arms. Seeing that the little man had no arms, the Scarecrow believed the little fellow harmless.

"I am sorry," said the Scarecrow; "but we must pass over your hill."

As quick as lightning the man's head shot forward as his neck stretched out. The top of his head hit the Scarecrow and sent him tumbling down the hill.

"It isn't as *easy* as you think!" the Hammer-Head cried out.

A chorus of loud laughter came from the other rocks, and Dorothy saw hundreds of the armless Hammer-Heads upon the hillside. The Lion grew angry. He gave a loud roar and dashed up the hill. Again a hard head shot out and the Lion was sent

tumbling down the hill like his friend.

"We'll never get over this hill," Dorothy said sadly.

"Why not call the Winged Monkeys?" said the Tin Man. "You have the Golden Cap."

"Oh! I should have thought of that long ago," said Dorothy.

Dorothy put the Golden Cap on her head and the Winged Monkeys appeared. Dorothy asked the Monkeys to carry them to Glinda's castle. The Monkeys picked up the friends and flew at once to the land of the South.

The Monkeys set them down in front of a grand castle. There three young girls stood, dressed in pretty red uniforms trimmed with gold braid.

"We have come to see the Good Witch who rules here," said Dorothy.

"I will ask Glinda if she will see you," said one of the girls, and she went into the castle. After a few moments she returned, saying that Glinda would see Dorothy and her friends.

They followed the soldier girl into a big room. There the Good Witch of the South sat upon a throne of rubies. She was both beautiful and young. Her hair was a rich red in color. It fell in flowing curls over her shoulders.

"What can I do for you, my child?"

Dorothy told the Good Witch her story. And she finished by saying: "My *greatest* wish now is to return to Kansas."

"I will send you back," said Glinda, "but you must give me the Golden Cap in return."

"Willingly!" exclaimed Dorothy.

Then Glinda turned to the Scarecrow, the Tin Man, and the Lion, and asked: "What will you do after Dorothy has left us?"

"If I can get over the Hammer-Heads' hill," said the Scarecrow, "I will return to the Emerald City to rule."

"I would like to get back to the land of the Winkies," replied the Tin Man; "for they have asked me to be their ruler."

"Over the hill of the Hammer-Heads," said the Lion, "is a great wood. I should like to go there and live quite happily."

"I shall command the Winged Monkeys to carry each of you

to your homes. As for Dorothy, the Silver Shoes will carry her to any place in the world in a wink of an eye. Just knock the heels together three times and you will be home."

"If that is so," said Dorothy, "I shall go home at once."

She threw her arms around the Lion's neck and kissed him. She patted his big head gently. Then she kissed the Tin Man, who was weeping so hard that she was afraid he would rust. But she *hugged* the soft body of the Scarecrow in her arms for the longest time. She didn't kiss him because she was afraid she might smear his painted face with her tears.

Dorothy now took Toto up in her arms, and having said one last good-bye, she clapped the heels of her shoes together, saying: "Take me home to Aunt Em."

At once she was whirling through the air so fast that all she could see or feel was the wind whistling past her ears. Then she stopped so suddenly that she was rolled over in the grass several times before she knew where she was. At length, however, she sat up and looked about her.

"Goodness gracious!" she cried.

For she was sitting on the broad Kansas prairie, and just before her was the new farmhouse Uncle Henry had built after the cyclone. Uncle Henry was milking the cows in the barnyard. Toto had jumped out of her arms and was running toward the barn, barking joyfully.

Dorothy stood up and found she was in her stocking feet. The Silver Shoes had fallen off over the desert in her flight through the air.

Aunt Em had just come out of the house when she looked up and saw Dorothy running toward her.

"My darling child!" she cried. "Where in the world did you come from?"

"From the Land of Oz," said Dorothy, gravely. "And oh, Aunt Em, I'm so *glad* to be at home again!"

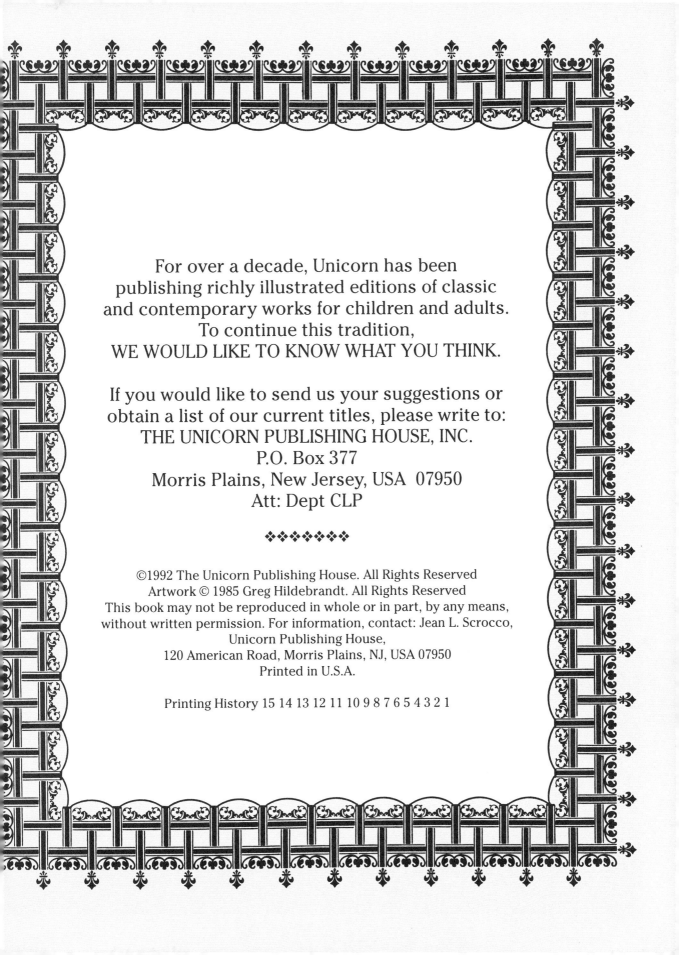

For over a decade, Unicorn has been
publishing richly illustrated editions of classic
and contemporary works for children and adults.
To continue this tradition,
WE WOULD LIKE TO KNOW WHAT YOU THINK.

If you would like to send us your suggestions or
obtain a list of our current titles, please write to:
THE UNICORN PUBLISHING HOUSE, INC.
P.O. Box 377
Morris Plains, New Jersey, USA  07950
Att: Dept CLP

❖❖❖❖❖❖❖